Introduction

My son, Abel, decided recently to become an actor. A difficult life, to be sure. One is more likely to fail than succeed. But it's what Abel wants and I support his decision.

As an actor myself, I felt there must be certain guideposts- do's and don'ts both obvious and subtle that I could share with my son to help him start out. Surprisingly, before I was done, I had compiled over a hundred! The next morning, as Abel was about to board the bus to take him to New York, or Los Angeles, I forget which, I placed my type-written suggestions into his hands and sent him into the world, a tear forming in my eye.

Somehow, these words made their way into print, the book you now hold in your hands. And when I see Abel up there on stage and in films, it gives me a glowing feeling, knowing I helped propel him there.

Enjoy!

♣ ACTOR'S LITTLE INSTRUCTION BOOK ♣

1. Avoid treating all the world as *your* stage.

♣ ACTOR'S LITTLE INSTRUCTION BOOK ♣

2. Concentrate more, act less.

3. Audition more. Talk less.

4. Pay your union dues.

♣ ACTOR'S LITTLE INSTRUCTION BOOK ♣

5. Audition well. Then, worry about getting the role.

6. Stop feeling stupid after auditions.

7. Send casting directors thank you notes.

♣ ACTOR'S LITTLE INSTRUCTION BOOK ♣

8. Know who you are auditioning for.

9. Research your role, don't fake it.

♣ ACTOR'S LITTLE INSTRUCTION BOOK ♣

10. Pay attention to your director.

11. Behave at rehearsals.

12. Bring donuts to dress rehearsals.

♣ ACTOR'S LITTLE INSTRUCTION BOOK ♣

13. Turn off the tv.

14. Have daily goals.

15. Save receipts.

♣ ACTOR'S LITTLE INSTRUCTION BOOK ♣

16. If your voice is an instrument, spend years learning to use it.

17. Learn a new dialect.

18. Watch foreign films.

♣ ACTOR'S LITTLE INSTRUCTION BOOK ♣

19. If you can imagine doing something else for a living, by all means do it.

♣ ACTOR'S LITTLE INSTRUCTION BOOK ♣

20. Read Stanislavski.

21. Read more plays.

22. Read the trade papers.

♣ ACTOR'S LITTLE INSTRUCTION BOOK ♣

23. Leave the dressing room cleaner than you found it.

24. Write down rehearsal notes.

25. Don't question your director. At least, not to his face.

♣ ACTOR'S LITTLE INSTRUCTION BOOK ♣

26. Treat your acting career as a business.

27. If you've got a $10 head, get a $10 headshot.

28. Expensive headshots are worthless sitting in a box.

♣ ACTOR'S LITTLE INSTRUCTION BOOK ♣

29. Don't lie on your resume.

30. Don't lie at auditions.

31. Don't lie to yourself.

♣ ACTOR'S LITTLE INSTRUCTION BOOK ♣

32. Call your parents today
    and tell them you're still an actor.

33. Encourage your family
    to be patrons of the arts.

34. Don't forget to love your family
    more than you love your art.

♣ ACTOR'S LITTLE INSTRUCTION BOOK ♣

35. If your agent's not working for you, you don't need to work for her.

36. If you're going to spend years in the business, don't spend minutes looking for a monologue.

♣ ACTOR'S LITTLE INSTRUCTION BOOK ♣

37. Just for today,
try smiling at people
who can't help you
with your career.

♣ ACTOR'S LITTLE INSTRUCTION BOOK ♣

38. Go see more plays.

39. An actor's education is never complete.

40. Approach mime cautiously.

♣ ACTOR'S LITTLE INSTRUCTION BOOK ♣

41. Arrive early.

42. Check your ego at the door.

43. Never say "I'm Sorry" after your monologue.

♣ **ACTOR'S LITTLE INSTRUCTION BOOK** ♣

44. Being an actor means not hesitating before admitting you're one.

♣ ACTOR'S LITTLE INSTRUCTION BOOK ♣

45. Make eye contact.

46. Pick up you cues.

47. Improvise.

♣ ACTOR'S LITTLE INSTRUCTION BOOK ♣

48. Read a scene with a friend.

49. Start a play reading group.

♣ ACTOR'S LITTLE INSTRUCTION BOOK ♣

50. Learn your lines ahead of schedule.

51. Never give a fellow actor honest advice, unless it's asked for. And never do it even then.

52. Remind yourself that what you do is just as important as a *real* job.

♣ **ACTOR'S LITTLE INSTRUCTION BOOK** ♣

53. Remember it is more important to deserve applause than receive it.

♣ ACTOR'S LITTLE INSTRUCTION BOOK ♣

54. Instead of saying, "Would you like some <u>butter</u> for your scone?", try "Would <u>you</u> like some butter for <u>your</u> scone?"

55. Don't, don't double emphasize.

♣ ACTOR'S LITTLE INSTRUCTION BOOK ♣

56. If you only audition for parts you're right for, you may miss a part you're right for.

57. At least once, sit in on auditions.

58. Don't be bullied into bad scripts.

♣ **ACTOR'S LITTLE INSTRUCTION BOOK** ♣

59. Don't wear buttons that say things like "Actor Person" or "Endangered Species: Working Actor."

♣ ACTOR'S LITTLE INSTRUCTION BOOK ♣

60. Keep your resume as clean and polished as your technique.

61. For a good stage name, use your middle name followed by the name of the first street you lived on.

♣ ACTOR'S LITTLE INSTRUCTION BOOK ♣

62. Correctly pronounce 'Anouilh,' 'Synge' and 'Mamet.'

63. Quote Shakespeare.

64. Let a foreign language contribute to your special skills.

♣ ACTOR'S LITTLE INSTRUCTION BOOK ♣

65. Say something short and anecdotal just before your monologue.

66. If you write your own monologues, don't admit it.

67. It isn't the size of the role, it's the size of the actor, and whether or not you look the part.

♣ ACTOR'S LITTLE INSTRUCTION BOOK ♣

68. Buy an answering machine.

69. Please don't perform on your answering machine.

♣ **ACTOR'S LITTLE INSTRUCTION BOOK** ♣

70. Create characters, not caricatures.

♣ ACTOR'S LITTLE INSTRUCTION BOOK ♣

71. Don't complain about delayed auditions.

72. Don't ignore your producer.

73. Don't break a leg.

♣ ACTOR'S LITTLE INSTRUCTION BOOK ♣

74. Keep track of every person in the business you meet.

75. Start your own mailing list.

76. Send nice notes to fellow actors who get great reviews.

♣ **ACTOR'S LITTLE INSTRUCTION BOOK** ♣

77. Be the easiest person
 in the cast
 to get along with.

♣ ACTOR'S LITTLE INSTRUCTION BOOK ♣

78. Read strange things aloud.

79. If your monologue feels strange, practice it in strange places.

80. If you're not in the moment, no one else will be.

♣ ACTOR'S LITTLE INSTRUCTION BOOK ♣

81. Practice for those Hollywood Parties by throwing your head back and laughing insanely.

82. Three Rules:
   1) Keep them on the line.
   2) Win-Win.
   3) First person to sell 100 subscriptions gets a coffee maker.

♣ ACTOR'S LITTLE INSTRUCTION BOOK ♣

83. Compliment the costume designer before your measurements are taken.

84. Compliment the stage manager before the first tech.

85. Practice looking sincere.

♣ **ACTOR'S LITTLE INSTRUCTION BOOK** ♣

86. Worry less about who else is doing your monologue and more about how well *you* do it.

♣ ACTOR'S LITTLE INSTRUCTION BOOK ♣

87. You don't need agents and directors who are mean.

88. Never let agents charge you for their services.

89. If it looks like a casting couch, don't sit down.

♣ ACTOR'S LITTLE INSTRUCTION BOOK ♣

90. Think actively when you think about your character.

91. Break the routine. Try singing your lines.

92. Review rehearsal notes.

♣ **ACTOR'S LITTLE INSTRUCTION BOOK** ♣

93. Bad reviews are just one person's opinion. Good reviews are universal.

♣ ACTOR'S LITTLE INSTRUCTION BOOK ♣

94. Have wealthy parents.

95. Get parents to think it was their idea to pay your rent.

96. Teach yourself to juggle.

♣ ACTOR'S LITTLE INSTRUCTION BOOK ♣

97. Every show should be better because you were a part of it.

98. Make a list of everything you love about acting and refer to it often.

99. Be selfish about your career.

♣ ACTOR'S LITTLE INSTRUCTION BOOK ♣

100. Be wary of advice from actors auditioning for the same part as you.

101. Always carry extra pictures and resumes.

102. The only thing to be said after your audition is "thank you."

♣ ACTOR'S LITTLE INSTRUCTION BOOK ♣

103. Be yourself.

♣ ACTOR'S LITTLE INSTRUCTION BOOK ♣

104. Learn to read music.

105. Learn to play an instrument.

106. Try writing a song.

♣ ACTOR'S LITTLE INSTRUCTION BOOK ♣

107. Try writing a play.

108. Adapt a bad 70's sitcom for the stage.

109. Watch old movies.

♣ ACTOR'S LITTLE INSTRUCTION BOOK ♣

110. Actors are like books; they can't be judged by their cover.

111. Avoid trying to be "cute" in your Playbill listing.

♣ ACTOR'S LITTLE INSTRUCTION BOOK ♣

112. Acting is repetition, so call your agent often.

113. Send a dozen casting directors something really funny.

♣ ACTOR'S LITTLE INSTRUCTION BOOK ♣

114. Remain passionate about your craft.

115. Enjoy your life in the theatre.

♣ ACTOR'S LITTLE DESTRUCTION BOOK ♣

115. Break a leg. Literally.

♣ ACTOR'S LITTLE DESTRUCTION BOOK ♣

112. If you forget photos, you can always draw a picture of yourself.

113. Explain to the casting director all thoughts, emotions and circumstances for the monologue you're about to do.

114. Put away a penny every time you talk about a part you should've gotten. Start shopping for a new car.

♣ ACTOR'S LITTLE DESTRUCTION BOOK ♣

109. Keep a list of everyone who's tried to hurt your acting career. When you've become rich and famous, squash them like the bugs they are.

110. Only attend workshops conducted by filthy rich actors.

111. Wake up. Headshots with eyepatches, vampire teeth and second heads are in!

♣ ACTOR'S LITTLE DESTRUCTION BOOK ♣

107. Trash the actor who got the part you were up for.

108. Ask yourself: If other actors aren't making you look good or buying the next round, why are you hanging around with them?

♣ ACTOR'S LITTLE DESTRUCTION BOOK ♣

104. Just after your character dies on stage, sneeze. It adds a human touch.

105. If you really want that stage kiss to look real, use your tongue.

106. Audiences will know you're 'good' if you can cry at will.

♣ ACTOR'S LITTLE DESTRUCTION BOOK ♣

102. Frontal nudity will get you noticed faster.

103. If you have stage fright, picture the audience naked. If you're really depraved, picture them with farm animals.

♣ ACTOR'S LITTLE DESTRUCTION BOOK ♣

100. Change your blocking on opening night.

101. Take an extra bow!

♣ ACTOR'S LITTLE DESTRUCTION BOOK ♣

97. Don't tell anyone
when you're performing.

98. Wear black and frequent coffee houses.

99. Drink Evian.

♣ ACTOR'S LITTLE DESTRUCTION BOOK ♣

95. Whisper while the director is giving notes.

96. If an actor doesn't buy you an opening night gift you have permission to sabotage his performance.

♣ ACTOR'S LITTLE DESTRUCTION BOOK ♣

94. Write a wacky one-person show about your dysfunctional family.

♣ ACTOR'S LITTLE DESTRUCTION BOOK ♣

92. Blow off researching your role.

93. If the show is bad, tell your friends it's performance art.

♣ ACTOR'S LITTLE DESTRUCTION BOOK ♣

90. Brush up on your ventriloquism.

91. Voice training is for actors afraid to sound like James Dean.

♣ ACTOR'S LITTLE DESTRUCTION BOOK ♣

88. Corner someone at a party and tell them how it feels being an actor.

89. Throw a party to celebrate your "walk-on" role in Unsolved Mysteries.

♣ ACTOR'S LITTLE DESTRUCTION BOOK ♣

85. Misspell directors names on your resume.

86. Select monologues from plays the director just directed.

87. Call the director and ask "Why didn't I get called back?"

♣ ACTOR'S LITTLE DESTRUCTION BOOK ♣

84. Treat your acting class as group therapy.

♣ ACTOR'S LITTLE DESTRUCTION BOOK ♣

82. Be sure to tell everyone how much you know about Restoration Drama.

83. Studied in England? Let everyone know.

♣ ACTOR'S LITTLE DESTRUCTION BOOK ♣

80. Classical monologues should always be done with your arm extending towards heaven, as if holding Yorick's skull.

81. Contemporary monologues should always be done with a slouch, a stutter and a toothpick.

♣ ACTOR'S LITTLE DESTRUCTION BOOK ♣

79. Good actors are the ones who win awards.

♣ ACTOR'S LITTLE DESTRUCTION BOOK ♣

76. Count the number of lines your part has. Don't take it if less than 25.

77. It's not the quality of the role, it's what you get to wear.

78. If you put your mind to it,
    you can do any role,
    especially your scene partner's.

♣ ACTOR'S LITTLE DESTRUCTION BOOK ♣

75. Give up.

♣ ACTOR'S LITTLE DESTRUCTION BOOK ♣

72. Blocking is for amateurs.

73. Eye contact is for actors afraid to stand on their own.

74. Remind the director what the play is "really" about.

♣ ACTOR'S LITTLE DESTRUCTION BOOK ♣

69. Once you've discovered the 'through-line' of your character, discard it and pose instead.

70. If you can't get a grasp of the character, do Jack Nicholson.

71. Make your characters bland yet dull. Force the audience to use their imaginations.

♣ ACTOR'S LITTLE DESTRUCTION BOOK ♣

66. Explain every single thought and feeling your character has to your fellow actors.

67. Ask for advice on a scene and then argue about it.

68. Give fellow actors "tips" on how to do the scene better.

♣ ACTOR'S LITTLE DESTRUCTION BOOK ♣

63. Accept money from understudies in exchange for getting sick.

64. Ask your agent if you can borrow money.

65. Staple money to your photo. It's a good way to get noticed.

♣ ACTOR'S LITTLE DESTRUCTION BOOK ♣

61. If they liked the show, they have taste. If they didn't, they're boobs.

62. When a critic pans your show, chalk it up to experience. Then, egg his house.

♣ ACTOR'S LITTLE DESTRUCTION BOOK ♣

58. When your character is not speaking, mug.

59. Why just be onstage when you can upstage.

60. For a touch of realism, upstage yourself.

♣ ACTOR'S LITTLE DESTRUCTION BOOK ♣

57. Remember, although you can always be replaced, they can't replace you before you've done a lot of damage.

♣ ACTOR'S LITTLE DESTRUCTION BOOK ♣

54. Typecast yourself.

55. Audition for roles twice your age.

56. Change your name.
    Men: Use natural words like 'Steel,' 'Stone' or 'Woody.'
    Women: Consult your spice rack.

♣ ACTOR'S LITTLE DESTRUCTION BOOK ♣

51. Perform your monologue directly to the auditioner.

52. Take four minutes to perform a two minute monologue.

53. Pause for a long time after your monologue so they can't tell if you're done.

♣ ACTOR'S LITTLE DESTRUCTION BOOK ♣

50. Start over half-way through your monologue.

♣ ACTOR'S LITTLE DESTRUCTION BOOK ♣

47. Wear leather pants and a torn t-shirt to a McDonald's commercial audition.

48. Point out how stupid the copy is at commercial auditions.

49. Stay up late power drinking before early morning calls.

♣ ACTOR'S LITTLE DESTRUCTION BOOK ♣

44. Keep stage managers on their toes by having them fetch things for you.

45. Call for lines at dress rehearsals.

46. Forget to show up to a performance or two.

♣ ACTOR'S LITTLE DESTRUCTION BOOK ♣

43. Ignore the business side of your acting career.

♣ ACTOR'S LITTLE DESTRUCTION BOOK ♣

40. Avoid standing directly in the lights.

41. Repeatedly ask technical people "Will this be ready by opening?"

42. Assume the stage manager's there to clean up after you.

♣ ACTOR'S LITTLE DESTRUCTION BOOK ♣

37. Mistreat props.

38. After the show closes, take props and costumes as keepsakes.

39. Tip the director on the way out.

♣ ACTOR'S LITTLE DESTRUCTION BOOK ♣

34. Don't prepare for cold readings.

35. Don't read. You're not a dramaturg.

36. Don't worry. Many fine actors have been discovered in chicken suits.

♣ ACTOR'S LITTLE DESTRUCTION BOOK ♣

31. Over-emphasize the lines they laugh at.

32. Point when saying 'You' and slap your chest when saying 'Me.'

33. Never allow an audience to affect your performance.

♣ ACTOR'S LITTLE DESTRUCTION BOOK ♣

30. No matter how many conflicts you have, reply 'none.'

♣ ACTOR'S LITTLE DESTRUCTION BOOK ♣

27. Paraphrase every line while the playwright is watching.

28. Tell a playwright he's the new Sam Shepard.

29. When the script says 'Exit,' that's just a request.

♣ ACTOR'S LITTLE DESTRUCTION BOOK ♣

24. Study exclusively with famous people.

25. Suck up to celebrities.

26. Name drop.

♣ ACTOR'S LITTLE DESTRUCTION BOOK ♣

22. Don't include a phone number on your resume.

23. Never update your resume, it's none of their business.

♣ ACTOR'S LITTLE DESTRUCTION BOOK ♣

21. Sacrifice your friends to get parts.

♣ ACTOR'S LITTLE DESTRUCTION BOOK ♣

19. If the director doesn't invite you to callbacks, assume it's a mistake and go anyway.

20. When you get to callbacks ask the director "Will this take long?"

♣ ACTOR'S LITTLE DESTRUCTION BOOK ♣

16. Misquote famous Shakespeare.

17. Rewrite that Shakespeare monologue to better suit your abilities.

18. Relieve the tedium of a Chekhov play with dribble glasses and poo-poo cushions.

♣ ACTOR'S LITTLE DESTRUCTION BOOK ♣

15. Take your art way too seriously.

♣ ACTOR'S LITTLE DESTRUCTION BOOK ♣

12. Brownnose.

13. Address the director as 'Your Worship.'

14. Laugh too loud and too long
    at everything your director says.

♣ ACTOR'S LITTLE DESTRUCTION BOOK ♣

9. Wear as much spandex as possible to auditions.

10. Wear "comedy & tragedy" accessories.

11. Refuse to wear your costume.

♣ ACTOR'S LITTLE DESTRUCTION BOOK ♣

8. If you can't act, teach. If you can't teach, write acting books.

♣ ACTOR'S LITTLE DESTRUCTION BOOK ♣

5. Memorize all the songs from Cats.

6. Talk endlessly about Andrew Lloyd Webber's current hit.

7. Sing show tunes at bars.

♣ ACTOR'S LITTLE DESTRUCTION BOOK ♣

2. Treat your agent with the same respect you'd give a postal employee.

3. Go exclusive with five agencies or more.

4. Hire your mom as your agent.

♣ ACTOR'S LITTLE DESTRUCTION BOOK ♣

1. Compromise your principles early and get it over with.

Introduction

I sat in my first acting class, reading the notes my father had written for me, and had a real hard time not laughing out loud. Oh sure, his suggestions were heartfelt and sincere, but this is the real world! I want to act, not hug people and feel good about myself.

In that class, I found myself scribbling in the margins, correcting his 'advice,' and in so doing, writing a potentially best-selling book.

I hope you enjoy the words you're about to read. I hope you find them helpful in your acting career. But most of all- I hope you've paid.

Love to all.

B.A. Mowrer, Jr.